A Spoon for Every Bite

To Lanette—
A smile for every day!
Joe Hayes

by Joe Hayes
illustrated by Rebecca Leer

ORCHARD BOOKS · NEW YORK

A Spoon for Every Bite

A LONG TIME AGO there was a poor couple who
lived in a small, tumbledown house. They were so poor that
they owned only two spoons—one for the husband and one
for the wife.

Their neighbor, on the other hand, was very rich.
His house was big and elegant and filled with fine furniture.
He was very proud of his wealth and his possessions, and he
lived in an extravagant way.

One year the poor couple had a baby, and when it was time to baptize the child, the wife said to her husband, "Why don't we ask our neighbor to be godfather to our baby?"

"But he is rich and we are poor," the man protested. "Why would he want to be our *compadre*?"

"You never know," said the wife. "He might accept. Maybe somehow it will change our luck."

So the poor man asked their rich neighbor to be their child's godfather, and the rich man accepted. They took the baby to the church to be baptized, and the neighbors became *compadres*.

The poor couple watched their baby grow rounder and more rosy cheeked with each passing week, and their hearts swelled with feelings of abundance.

One day the poor woman said to her husband, "Now that our neighbor is our *compadre*, I think we should invite him to eat supper with us this evening."

But the man asked, "How can we do that? We have only two spoons."

So they didn't invite the rich man for supper that day. Instead, they began to save their pennies until at last they could afford to buy a third spoon. Then the poor man went to the rich man's house and invited his *compadre* to come for dinner.

The poor woman made a very tasty soup, and when the two men arrived, she sat the rich man at the place with the shiny new spoon. "This is your place, *compadre*," she said. "You get to use our third spoon. We just bought it today."

The rich man could scarcely believe what he heard. "Do you mean to say you own only three spoons?" he asked.

"Oh, yes," the poor man told his *compadre*. "Until this morning we had only two spoons, but we bought a new one today so that you could join us for dinner."

The rich man couldn't contain himself. He laughed aloud. "You had only two spoons! And you bought a new one for me to eat with! Why," he boasted, "I have so many spoons in my house I could use a different one each day of the year if I wished to."

The poor man was embarrassed
and annoyed by his *compadre*'s
boastfulness. But the poor woman spoke
right up in reply. "Oh, that's nothing,
compadre," she said. "We have a friend in
these parts who uses a different spoon for every
bite he eats. He never uses the same spoon twice."

The rich man waved his hand in disbelief. But the
poor man gave his wife a knowing wink and swore that it was
true. "My wife is telling the truth, *compadre*," he said. "Our
friend uses a different spoon for every single bite he eats."

The rich man was so upset by the idea that
someone lived even more lavishly than he did that he
could hardly eat his soup.

That night he lay awake thinking about it.

The next day the rich man's servant came running to the poor man's house. "What did you give my master to eat last night?" he demanded.

The poor man shrugged. "He ate the same thing we all ate—the tastiest soup my wife has ever made. Why do you ask?"

"Your soup must have driven him crazy. This morning at breakfast he insisted on using a different spoon for every bite he ate. And after he took one bite from a spoon, he ordered me to get rid of it."

The poor *compadre* laughed to himself. This was just the kind of thing he and his wife had hoped would happen. "And what does your master tell you to do with the spoons you're ordered to get rid of?"

"I asked what should be done with them," the servant replied. "And my master laughed and said, 'Give them to my *compadres*. They have only three spoons!'"

At his noonday meal the rich man did the same thing, and he did the same at dinner as well. That evening the rich man's servant carried a pile of spoons to the poor couple's house and left them beside the door.

The next day was no different. The rich man insisted on a new spoon for every bite. The same thing happened the following day and the day after. In less than a week the servant informed the rich man that there were no more spoons left in the house. "Get me some more!" growled the rich man. "Do you think I'm too poor to buy more spoons?"

His servant hurried to the store. When the rich man had used up all the spoons in town, the servant had to travel to stores in other towns.

Soon the rich man began selling his
livestock and land just to buy more spoons.
A mountain of spoons stood beside the
poor couple's house.

At the end of a year the rich man had squandered all his wealth. And there were just three spoons in his house. He walked angrily to the poor couple's house and pounded on the door.

"You lied to me!" he roared when they opened it. "No one can use a new spoon for every bite he eats. I have proved it. I am the richest man for miles around, and not even I can use a spoon for only one bite."

"No, *compadre*," the poor man said calmly. "You're mistaken. Our friend does just what we said."

"That's right," added the poor woman. "Day in and day out, year in and year out, he uses a different spoon for every bite he eats."

"Take me to meet this friend of yours," the rich man demanded. "He must be the wealthiest man in the world."

The poor couple took their *compadre* to the nearby Indian pueblo. They went to the house of the poor couple's friend. The Indian and his wife welcomed the *compadres* and invited them to stay and have a meal.

"That's just what I came for," said the rich man. "I want you to show me how you use a new spoon for every bite you eat."

"Spoon?" asked the Indian. "This is the only spoon I
use." He pointed to a stack of tortillas on the table. "That's
the spoon my people have used since the beginning of time."

He broke off a piece of tortilla and scooped up some
beans. The beans and the spoon disappeared into his mouth.

"He'll never use that spoon again," laughed the poor
man.

Again the rich man was too upset to eat his meal. He got
up from the table and walked sadly home.

But the poor couple enjoyed every bite the Indian shared
with them—spoon and all. And then they walked home smiling.
They knew that when they had sold all the spoons their rich *compadre*
had thrown away, they would live out their days in comfort.

A NOTE FOR READERS AND STORYTELLERS

In telling this story, I have combined two elements of the Hispanic story tradition of the Southwest. The deceptive reference to the use of a tortilla as an eating utensil is cast in the form of a picaresque tale featuring two *compadres*, one poor but clever and the other rich and overbearing.

Several brief tales and *chistes* hinge on the tortilla as a spoon that is used only once. From a high school teacher I heard a Mexican version in which a proud *conquistador* brags to a humble Indian that his king eats off plates of silver and gold. Feigning indifference, the Indian replies that his chief is so rich he uses a different spoon for every bite. In an Anglo-American variant a seasoned traveler on the Santa Fe Trail yarns a greenhorn about the high style of life in New Mexico with the same idea. The joke is well-known to the old ones in New Mexico. On one occasion as I told my version at *El Rancho de las Golondrinas* Historical Museum south of Santa Fe, I noticed an elderly Hispanic gentleman in the group turn toward his wife when I said the phrase ''a spoon for every bite'' and silently mouth the word *tortilla*.

Humorous tales about rich and poor *compadres* abound in Hispanic story lore. In his compendious collection of Spanish narrative in the Southwest, *Cuentos españoles de Colorado y Nuevo Méjico*, Juan B. Rael dedicates an entire section to *los dos compadres*, and many stories that are otherwise categorized involve two individuals identified as *compadres—el uno rico, el otro muy pobre*. In one such tale, the tortilla/spoon joke is briefly repeated.

Curiously, while the old tales so often portray an almost adversarial relationship between *compadres*, the actual relationship is quite the opposite. The role of godparent is highly esteemed, and parents typically choose a very dear friend to fill it. The tales of *los dos compadres*, however, are quite old and perhaps reflect the time when the wealthy *hacendado* would serve as godfather to all the children born to his *peones* as an expression of noblesse oblige. Whatever the true reason may be, these tales serve as a reminder that folktales cannot always be viewed as accurate expressions of the contemporary mores and practices of the culture from which they derive.

For all the readers who are rich in friendship, love, and happiness—J.H.   For my parents—R.L.

Text copyright © 1996 by Joe Hayes. Illustrations copyright © 1996 by Rebecca Leer. First Orchard Paperbacks edition 1999. All rights reserved. No part of this book may be reproduced or transmitted in any form or by any means, electronic or mechanical, including photocopying, recording, or by any information storage or retrieval system, without permission in writing from the Publisher. Orchard Books, A Grolier Company, 95 Madison Avenue, New York, NY 10016

Manufactured in the United States of America. Printed and bound by Phoenix Color Corp. Book design by Mina Greenstein. The text of this book is set in 14 point Meridien Roman. The illustrations are pastel reproduced in full color. Hardcover 10 9 8 7 6 5 4 3 2   Paperback 10 9 8 7 6 5 4 3 2 1

Library of Congress Cataloging-in-Publication Data. Hayes, Joe. A spoon for every bite / by Joe Hayes ; illustrated by Rebecca Leer.   p.   cm.   Summary: A poor husband and wife ask their rich neighbor to be godfather of their child, and once they are compadres, prey upon his pride and extravagance to trick him out of his fortune. ISBN 0-531-09499-5 (tr.) ISBN 0-531-08799-9 (lib. bdg.) ISBN 0-531-07143-X (pbk.)   [1. Wealth—Fiction. 2. Pride and vanity—Fiction.]   I. Leer, Rebecca, ill.   II. Title. PZ7.H31474Sp 1996 [E]—dc20 95-22019